Build-a-Bimbo Heroine: Miracle Girl

The Silver Queen's Superharem, Volume 2

Layla Rose

Published by Comfy Cotton Underthings Publishing, 2022.

BUILD-A-BIMBO HEROINE: MIRACLE GIRL

First edition. October 31, 2022.

ISBN: 979-8201040802

Written by Layla Rose.

Table of Contents

Thanks to everyone who has supported my odd little journey as a bimbo writer.

Thanks to everyone who has become part of my cozy little Discord community.

And once again, thank you to WrenZephyr for the amazing cover art!

Prologue: A Suitable Nemesis

The Silver Queen, born Emily Snow, had it all. That happened when you had the power to warp reality. Some people in her position might have become heroes, but that would have been a waste. Heroes tried to do everything for a "greater good," and that lacked creativity. Emily could have *everything*. Limits meant nothing to her. She was perfectly equipped to be a villain.

The Silver Queen never regretted her career path. She had money, influence, and power. She had conquered and dominated the world just to reset it when she got bored.

The one thing The Silver Queen lacked, it seemed, was a true Nemesis. There were heroes who stood against her in theory, of course, but none of them wanted to cross her. The Silver Queen was unopposed. A good villainess deserved a nemesis that served as her foil to contrast her imposing malevolence. Not having one was a slight to her otherwise sterling reputation.

She could turn one of the world's greatest heroes into her zealous enemy by planting the idea in their head. The Queen researched the rosters of the Revengers, the Honor Guild, and every two-bit West Coast team heroes were pumping out quarterly. She took a handful of headliners for a spin on a trial basis, but ultimately cut them all loose.

None of the current working heroes fit the bill. Publicly, they were beacons of virtue, but thematically, they lacked what she was looking for in a foil.

The Silver Queen was defined by the miraculous gifts she was bestowed and how she chose to use them. She was unabashedly selfish. She needed a nemesis who was given miracles of her own and felt a calling to use them selflessly.

If none of the heroes were up to the task of being her nemesis, The Silver Queen would create her own. Not a competent one, of course; another defining trait of The Silver Queen was that she always won. If her nemesis was to be her foil, she would have to be destined to lose.

Until that eventual fall, The Queen would have fun embarrassing her greatest enemy. It had been months since she turned the vigilante Blackwing into her bimbo pet, Princess. The omnipotent reality-warper was itching to have her fun toying with a new bright-eyed idealist.

THE TARGET WAS PICKED at random. Jeanie Gray was an unassuming, rather plain woman living her own quiet life as a reporter. Reporters made good heroes; they had romanticized opinions on truth, and their work naturally gave them the flexibility to fuck off and deal with an intergalactic incident if necessary.

After a week of observing the well-mannered young woman working, Emily was satisfied with her choice. The Queen warped reality, changing the fabric of Jeanie's DNA to set her plan in motion.

Without knowing why or how, one day the redheaded reporter woke up and realized there was a change in her. The world around her was more vibrant and she could feel power coursing through her veins.

The Silver Queen wanted her power set to be iconic, with the obvious stipulation that Jeanie could not read or influence the mind of her greatest nemesis.

Emily set the wheel in motion, stoking Jeanie's sense of justice. She always envied people with the power to do real good in the world, so pushing her to become a do-gooder hero took almost no manipulation on the Queen's part!

Jeanie was granted a miracle in the form of her new powers, so she would take on the moniker of Miracle Girl. Why she was granted such amazing gifts, she could not say, but it was on her to understand her new purpose as a heroine.

The villainess would leave Jeanie be for a few months so she could build Miracle Girl's reputation as a heroine. Once she got a handle of her psychic powers, Jeanie could quickly make a name for herself as one of the true powerhouses in the hero world.

Emily could be patient; part of the game was building sweet, sweet anticipation. She would watch Jeanie earn her accolades, becoming a true hero of the people. That would be when her plan would set into motion. A swift rise to glory would make her slow fall from grace all the more satisfying.

The Silver Queen wanted Miracle Girl to be loved and respected before the reality-bender had her fun turning the heroine into a total bimbo laughingstock.

Chapter 1: A Hero's Hips Don't Lie

en Months Later.

Jeanie Gray lived a blessed life. At twenty-six, her work as a reporter was finally getting recognized, her peers were starting to respect her, and secretly, she was a *motherfucking superhero!*

The powers appeared without warning one day. As an avid fan of the world's superheroes, Jeanie was quick to test out her powers. Through a week of self-discovery, she learned how to use her newfound telekinesis, pyrokinesis, and even telepathy! Whatever mysterious force gave her those new gifts, they were not messing around; she was dealing with some big-ticket superpowers.

People were apprehensive of *another* New York superheroine, but Miracle Girl was sure to prove herself with one impressive victory after another. The news reported on her, and as a reporter, she even reported on herself sometimes.

The moment that truly made her star was the only "win" the heroine did not consider a true victory. The Silver Queen, one of the world's most intimidating villains, summoned a full-on kaiju monster in the heart of Manhattan. New York's other heroes were mysteriously missing, but Miracle Girl showed up on the scene! She contained the monster's fire blasts and turned them back on the giant reptile.

With the great mental strain, Jeanie somehow lifted the dinosaur with her telepathy. With the world watching, she dragged the monster far into the sky and tossed it out of the Earth's atmosphere! Her head was left spinning and she knew she lacked the strength to fight The Silver Queen, but she stood to challenge her anyway for the sake of the city.

And somehow, The Silver Queen decided it was time to retreat. She smirked and disappeared, but not before loudly proclaiming the young heroine as her nemesis; the only hero brave and foolish enough to stand up to her.

After that day, the people saw Miracle Girl as a beacon of hope for the city. Jeanie wanted to deliver on that faith, valuing her own image for the first time in her career. When she stopped a crime, she used her telepathy to make sure no one remembered the exact details of her freckled face, but she had them remember Miracle Girl. She wanted them to remember how she saved them and how the hero made them feel.

TODAY'S CRIMINALS WERE bank robbers. No impressive powers or global pedigree; just masked, armed bank robbers.

Truthfully, the crime was garden variety and arguably beneath a hero of her standing, but that was the point; no crime was too small for Miracle Girl. If citizens were in danger, that was enough reason for her to show up!

Miracle Girl landed gracefully, adorned in green leather and a golden sash. She pushed the door of the bank open with her mind, making her grand entrance!

Before any criminal could point a gun at her or the hostages, Jeanie knocked them all out of their hands with a mental wave. Jeanie took confident strides toward the thugs, who were hesitant to charge her without weapons. They were bigger and physically stronger, but they knew who she was. They had to take her seriously.

This was shaping up like every other non-powered crime Jeanie effortlessly stopped, but an unexpected tingle changed everything.

Jeanie felt the peculiar tingle running up and down her spine, like a pleasurable shiver. The feeling settled in her midsection. The intensity of the tingling made her stop in her tracks as her legs went weak.

A moan escaped against Jeanie's will and the change was almost instantaneous. The bones, muscles, and fat making up Jeanie's hips and upper thighs all shifted outward. Her lean, almost lanky frame filled out as her new jiggly thighs and padded hips strained the leather of her pants, opening small tears across the fabric.

Jeanie tried to take a few more steps forward, still wobbling from the after-effects of the change. She could feel a change in the rhythm of her walk. The sway of her hips wasn't just noticeable, it was absurd. Each step, she couldn't help but swing from one side to the other.

A robber laughed, confirming her fear that it was, in fact, that bad. "Oh no, watch out guys. Miracle Bitch is gonna sexy walk over and kick our asses." The rest of his crew joined in the laughter, happy to make light of the hero opposing them.

Jeanie groaned, wondering why her normally unassuming figure had a new set of curves. That barely did it justice, with her hips jutting out to twice the width of her waist! Did this change have something to do with her powers? They showed up unexpectedly as well, but childbearing hips were a far cry from pyrokinesis?

Jeanie would have to give that some thought later because that robber was right. Just because she was going to sashay obscenely with each step didn't mean it would stop her from kicking their asses.

The unconscious criminals were handed off to the police and reporters arrived on the scene after Jeanie departed, but some of the hostages had phones. Photos of Miracle Girl's new silhouette were circulating on the internet by evening.

EMILY PET PRINCESS' hair, letting the fuckpet under her desk happily lick her pussy while she perused the photos of her handywork online. It was a small first alteration, but it made her grin wickedly; after almost a year of patiently waiting, her game had officially begun.

Chapter 2: Caked-Up Crimefighter

Okay, so it took some time for Jeanie to get used to her new hips. As a hero, she could hover around, but even outside of costume, people giggled or stared when she walked. Her co-workers whispered about her new frame, wondering if she just hid them with the clothes she wore or if she had some kind of experimental plastic surgery.

She was still unsure why the Miracles, or whatever mysterious force kept blessing her with them, thought she needed cartoonishly wide hips. After sitting on the question for a few days, she ultimately decided not to question whatever cosmic force was so kind to her in the first place. At least it made her silhouette more recognizable?

AFTER TAILORING A NEW, more forgiving set of leather pants, Jeanie could squeeze herself back into her costume with patience and the help of a belt hidden under her signature sash. Finally dressed, Jeanie could jump into action and answer the call to deal with a gang of B-List villains.

The Fraternity was another group of low-powered lowlifes whose main claim to fame was their attitude. The bad guy boys' club loved to get raucous and pig-headed, particularly when a woman had the misfortune of roving into their general area.

Today, that unfortunate woman was the mayor, though that involved less roving and more kidnapping.

After breaking into their underground club house, Miracle Girl quickly torched one of their old couches and tossed it at Speedo and Tadpole, knocking them out the moment the fight started. The two members with brain cells realized what was going on and snatched up the mayor, trying to retreat into the halls of their base.

Miracle Girl gave chase, choosing to run rather than float through the confined space. She was hot on the tail of the two Fraternity goons. The Big Guy carried the mayor in one arm while Earthshaker broke the shitty flooring of their clubhouse, pulling out boulders from the ground to lob at Miracle Girl. Easy! She telekinetically caught the boulder and tossed it back at the unexpecting villain.

He managed to stop the boulder with another at the last second. Changing his plan, he created obstacles to make it harder for Miracle Girl to keep up. "Slowing down? Guess those fuck-me hips ain't too aerodynamic!"

Jeanie groaned, pushing herself to run even faster, not stopping when she felt a tingling sensation coursing through her lower body. Slowly, unbeknownst to her, Jeanie's ass grew in size, with fatty cells multiplying and expanding. Each quick step added another pound of flesh, ballooning out her barely contained cheeks until—

RIIIIP!

Jeanie was shocked by the sound and how close it was, but she could not stop. She had to focus on her mission, ignoring a sudden rush of cool air hitting her body. She had to run harder, and as she did, her newly exposed cheeks clapped loudly with each step.

Each clap was louder than the last until each clap created a small shockwave. The ripples grew more intense until one shockwave was finally enough to knock the villains off their feet.

The Big Guy fell on top of Earthshaker, dropping the Mayor and functionally taking them both out. Once The Big Guy was down, it was a whole project to get him back to his feet.

Jeanie telepathically put the weakened villains to sleep when she caught up with them. The mayor scrambled to her feet to thank her, but when Jeanie looked over her shoulder, the mayor's eyes were fixated on the heroine's new absolute shelf of an ass.

Was that why her last Miracle gave her obscene hips? To help her accommodate a fat new ass and the... odd power it came with? The Miracles truly worked in mysterious ways. This was not exactly a power she was going to be able to use in her costume normally, but... well, it did save the day today?

Maybe the Miracles knew what they were doing, but she just hoped their next gift wouldn't ruin her pants.

Chapter 3: All Torn Up and Ready to Show

This was the third time in two weeks.

Miracle Girl went out to deal with three different villains over the course of two weeks, and EVERY TIME she got into a scrape with some baddies, her costume suffered the consequences.

Tonight's throwdown pitted her against the terroristic villain Acid Spitter. He was a particularly nasty one, crashing a big fancy gala event in hopes of burning up a room full of rich people with personally developed acid. The concoction would melt away clothes, flesh, and bones until nothing was left but their jewels.

His antics were easy enough for Miracle Girl to deal with thanks to her Miracles. He released a burst of acid in her direction, but her telekinesis manifested itself in an invisible barrier!

The thin telekinetic layer of protection wrapped tightly around her skin, shielding her from the caustic chemicals, giving her the chance to clear the ballroom by collecting the thick fumes into a telekinetic bubble along with their creator and tossing them out the window. Leave it to the Miracles to give her the perfect gift to make her skin impervious to harm!

Her costume was not afforded that luxury of protection. Despite her best efforts to be careful, by the time the police arrived to handcuff the villain, she barely had a costume left at all.

Losing another costume was going to be a hassle. They were not cheap and the tailor she ordered from was going to get suspicious. This incident was frustrating, but... well, that was not the feeling Jeanie was focusing on in the moment.

With party guests, police, and even news cameras gathered on the lawn, Miracle Girl was the only thing anyone could look at. Jeanie should get out of sight, especially with her clothes reduced to tatters, barely clinging to her body. Barely anything remained to hide her modest chest, and her dumptruck of an ass was on full display yet again. Staying on the scene was inappropriate.

Despite that, Jeanie was lingering because feeling all those eyes on her did something. Jeanie felt a new tingling feeling. It wasn't like the Miracle tingles, not exactly. Nothing about her body was changing; she did a thorough check to make sure.

This tingling sensation was centered squarely between her legs. Being a hero meant constantly ending up as the center of attention, but this was new. Her body was all anyone cared about, and as they drank in her exposed skin, Jeanie realized it was filling a deep, intense need she never noticed before.

When Jeanie finally returned to her apartment, she gave that spot between her legs the attention it deserved. The entire time she played with her clit, she was thinking of those eyes and cameras watching her body. She pictured them watching her now, as she pulled a rubber dildo from her dresser and filled herself with it. The idea of people seeing her in her supposedly shameful throes of passion made the young heroine cum instantly. This uncharacteristically lewd desire was so tempting;

it was guaranteed to become her bedside fantasy for the foreseeable future.

Not that she would go that far. Still, maybe it wasn't the *worst* thing that her costumes couldn't seem to make it to the end of a mission...

Chapter 4: Bold New Style

The Silver Queen watched the evening news with religious consistency. She was vain enough to enjoy the anxious reports of her own mischief, but even on her days off, it was good to know which heroes deserved to get knocked down a peg or two. The Queen was nothing if not a master at pegging heroes, after all.

Recently, she took malicious joy in watching the confused reporting of her newest pet project, Miracle Girl. The golden girl was rarely out of the limelight since Emily intentionally lifted her into the public eye, but recent events changed the public perception of the heroine from worship to speculation.

Miracle Girl was still a powerful and respected hero, but even the news was pointing out how her costumes were always in suggestive tatters by the time they arrived to the scene. Less reputable news stations even made comments about the sudden and possibly intentional boost to the heroine's butt. The goodie-two-shoes of crime fighting developing a naughty streak was good for ratings, so any further lewd developments would be guaranteed to stay in the primetime spotlight.

And oh, if that thought didn't make The Silver Queen want to cum right then and there. Which she did, into the waiting mouth of Princess. The ex-heroine always dutifully served the Queen from under her desk with her head wedged between

Emily's thighs while she enjoyed the news, like the good lapdog she was.

Things were going so well, maybe it was time to whisper a suggestion into Miracle Girl's head. Nothing too overpowering; she just needed a nudge to embrace what she already knew deep down.

JEANIE WAS STILL GOING through costumes like tissue paper. With the way they disintegrated in every fight, maybe that was what they were secretly made of.

The constant destruction of her clothes should have been frustrating, but every time, without fail, she was soaking what was left of her panties standing there in the aftermath. Depending on how the suit was torn, she bet onlookers could even tell she was dripping, and that was even hotter.

Something about people seeing more of her was more satisfying than any sex she had thus far in her sheltered life. Maybe that was another sign from the Miracles. After her most recent pair of mangled pants, she decided to stop fighting the good feelings and reinterpreted her look.

With her new hips and ass, pants a huge pain in the... well, ass. It took minutes of effort and strain just to squeeze her massive dumper into a pair of pants she was just going to ruin anyway. They weren't offering her any protection, with her telekinetic barrier protecting her exposed skin regardless. If she was getting more enjoyment from her costume when it was torn up and covering less of her, maybe it was time to cut out the middleman.

Changing into her new costume was a much quicker process. She got a pair of high-cut brief bottoms that were stretchy enough to pull over her hips and ass, freeing her thighs from their suffocating constraints while covering, at most, a quarter of Jeanie's cheeks. She tossed a green skirt over her briefs, but it was mostly for decoration; the skirt was barely wider than belt holding it in place under her sash.

Looking at herself in the mirror, Jeanie had another epiphany: if she was changing her bottoms, why not just go for an entirely new look? Her new top not only exposed her midriff, but it also even came with a window formed by the cups of the top and the collar where her straps met around her neck. Boob windows had a long, proud history in the hero world, so why not lean into it?

Content with her look, Miracle Girl patrolled intensely, looking for any excuse to make a scene and get attention. After busting up a run-of-the-mill jewelry store heist, she waited around for the first reporters to arrive—and once they got there, more followed suit *very quickly*.

Some reporters tried to ask her serious questions about the non-powered criminals, but eventually one of the sleezier news sites on the scene asked about her outfit. "So, is this like... a Summer look? Things just a little too hot, or...?"

Miracle Girl grinned, her chest puffed out proudly, putting her modest cleavage on full display. "I thought it was time to embrace a new attitude. I want to feel confident and empowered, and I ultimately decided this was the style that I find the most pleasure—er, comfort in." She beamed, knowing the cameras were watching her dazzling smile but the cameramen were watching wetness slipping down her exposed inner thighs.

She DID feel empowered, and she wanted everyone to know it.

All those other lewd feelings could stay her little secret.

Chapter 5: Busting Out

If Emily had any sense of morals, incepting an idea into Jeanie's head to alter her good girl personality would be a clear offense. Fortunately, morals were boring and a supervillainess could gladly forgo them and enjoy a press conference from her tarted-up nemesis.

Look at her, putting herself on display so proudly. Emily gave her the nudge, but that vanity was deep in Jeanie, under her meek insecurity. She barely needed The Silver Queen's help to stand proudly before the public, trying not to rub her needy thighs together.

What she could use The Silver Queen's help was that lackluster rack. She puffed it out so proudly, but a heroine of her caliber did not deserve to represent the Itty Bitty Titty Committee. It was cliché, but maybe it was finally time for Emily to break out a fan favorite "Miracle" for Jeanie.

MIRACLE GIRL WAS BUILDING a name for herself, through it was a very specific name. New stations liked to talk about her, but while some of them still treated her as a beacon of hope, others saw an opportunity to talk about how she was more sex symbol than hero.

That was so dumb! Okay, did it make her want to masturbate? Yes, but when she was done, she was still miffed. Why did it matter what she wore if she was doing her job as a hero? She was still one of the best in the business when it came to stopping crime, even if no one wanted to take her seriously when she used her ass-clap shockwaves to save the day.

Let the media talk! Miracle Girl had a job to do, and today that meant a second chance to stand up to her nemesis.

Miracle Girl landed in front of Sterk Industries, where the mysterious Silver Queen had made an appearance, according to the police radios and news reports. Jeanie was sure she landed at the right spot, looking at the address where Sterk Industries was supposed to be, but all she saw was... a nightclub?

"Those ridiculous hips must slow you down, girlie. You're late."

Miracle Girl looked up and blinked as her eyes adjusted to the flashing neon lights to see the stunning blonde woman descending from the rooftop dancefloor to meet her. Reporters were on the scene from a safe distance, wishing they could be close enough to listen, but knowing no one wanted to be close enough to earn the Queen's attention.

"Sterk was positioning himself to be a serious business rival," The Silver Queen admitted, giving credit to the billionaire playboy philanthropist behind the Titanium Man persona. "Fortunately, that won't be an issue now. Not when all of Sterk Industries best and brightest have been reduced to bubbly party girls. I'm sure a tech bro like him will like them better this way anyway."

Miracle Girl pouted, trying to read Silver Queen's mind to find some way to undo her mischief. Maybe that would have been the easy way out, but much to her chagrin, her attempts came back empty. Something about the powerful evildoer locked her mind away from Jeanie's sight.

"Undo your damage or I'll have to bust you up, Queenie!" Jeanie felt righteous anger swelling in her chest. And a tingle. So much tingling, her eyes went wide and the heroine moaned. No, no, not in front of her nemesis!

Her eyes abandoned the villain, looking down to watch as her modest breasts swelled like balloons being inflated. She wrapped her arms around them as her growing tits mashed together, popping free of their cups until they were fighting to share every inch of her costume's boob window. Each new pound of flesh sent a new wave of pleasure coursing through Jeanie's body, making it hard to focus

The Silver Queen smirked, watching Jeanie's legs wobble until she buckled and fell to her knees. The distant cameras saw hands trying to cover her breasts, but Emily could see the heroine was frantically groping herself. "Maybe you should be concerned with your own bust. I'll leave you to your own titillating tribulations, Miracle Girl. Til next time." And with a wink, The Silver Queen vanished into thin air.

Miracle Girl's vision finally came back into focus when the growing mercifully stopped and the pleasure subsided. As her head started clearing up, she anxiously looked around for any sign of her target. Dammit! The Queen got away.

Miracle Girl was left alone, at least until reporters ran in from their hiding places and scantily-clad go-go girls shuffled out of the city's newest nightclub. She had to admit to her first true defeat to the media with her G-cup titties spilling out of her B-cup costume.

She would feel ashamed if the whole affair did not leave her so horny.

Chapter 6: Obviously Arousing Adornments

Jeanie's excessively televised loss to The Silver Queen was dominating the news waves for a whole week after the incident. Did the city really not have better things to report on? She worked so hard to be a hero, but every sexist reporter and talking head in town was mocking her for her impromptu breast augmentation and the witness reports of "horny fondling."

The best thing to do was turn off the news until they stopped acting like tabloids. Miracle Girl had to focus on doing her job as a hero. If she kept that up, they would have something new to report on.

A flashy crime would have been great for media attention, but not every fight had to be some intense chase or battle of superpowers. Some crime required a discrete, intelligent approach. Fortunately for Jeanie, she was an investigative journalist.

Criminals were whispering about a seedy casino in the city that had possible ties to The Silver Queen. Justice was her priority, but after what happened at Sterk Industries, (now the Boom-Boom Room,) Jeanie had to admit she would relish the possibility of some well-deserved revenge.

Miracle Girl used her telepathy to sneak past a guard, putting her in the position to sneak around the back halls of the Casino. There was something exhilarating about playing at spy work, even if Miracle Girl had powers to fall back on. She kept her footsteps light and her lips sealed tight, not wanting to draw attention to herself.

That was the plan, at least, but keeping her lips sealed was proving to be surprisingly difficult.

When she moved, the cups of her costume top brushed her nipples in a way that was setting off sirens in her head and her briefs. A hero's willpower and discipline were evidently not enough to stop sharp gasps of surprise at each burst of sensation.

Jeanie had to find a corner to hide in to give herself a break, because all this brushing was unbearable and she needed to recollect herself. Nothing about this costume was different than her last outfit, so something was amiss.

Jeanie had to know what was causing so many sudden problems, so she sacrificed modesty and pulled her cups down to take a look at her breasts. They were just as massive as she remembered, but she was sure when she put on her costume, her nipples didn't have big silver bars with emerald pierced through them. Looking past her breasts, which was a challenge in and of itself,) she had a matching bellybutton ring, too!

Jeanie inspected one of the bars, looking for a divide where she could pull them apart and remove them until her mission was over. No dice; the bar was one solid cylinder of metal, and the studs on either end were too long to pull through. The moment Jeanie tried, her vision flashed white from the intense pleasure from her nipple and a lewd groan slipped out.

Was this really another Miracle? What would piercings do to make her a better hero?

Frustrated, Miracle Girl tried to get back to sneaking around and snooping for clues, but her nipples were hard as little rocks so apparent, they were visible through the fabric of her top. The constant brushing against the fabric led to unintentional mewling, and by the time she got to the back office, the mewling was moaning, and a room of nearby thugs easily overheard her and ran to meet her.

One brutish man smirked at her, his eyes and every other set of eyes in the room glued on her tits. "Too cold in here for you, Miracle Bitch?"

Miracle Girl sighed, feeling the flushing of her cheeks from the attention and the *constant, overwhelming pleasure.* She accepted what she was going to have to do until she had a better solution, pulling her top down. Her heavy breasts bounced free and the gang of assholes howled and whistled.

Criminals watching her bare tits made her horny, but it was infinitely more manageable than her sensitive nipples.

Miracle Girl igniting a flame around her balled-up fist. If she had to take out her frustration on anyone, this room of disrespectful thugs was a good start.

Chapter 7: Miraculous Beauty

The latest photos of Miracle Girl in the newspaper made The Silver Queen smile. After yet another costume change, most newspapers had to edit a censor bar over the heroine's chest because the "window" on her costume had expanded. The shoulder straps of her costume no longer connected to cups, but green harness straps that framed each unexposed tit. The uncensored photos circulating online introduced the public to Miracle Girl's new permanent body jewelry.

Miracle Girl's reputation was taking a hasty turn from "noble beacon of virtue" to "horny exhibitionist embarrassment." The Silver Queen's plan was in full motion, but she did not want her idealist idiot getting discouraged. Jeanie needed encouragement; a reminder that there was a path, even if she could not see where it was leading her.

JEANIE ALWAYS BELIEVED the Miracles were gifts to help her save people. She started her journey as a hero with confidence in her purpose, but after so many... unorthodox Miracles, she was conflicted. Some of the Miracles gave her powers, but others were just changing the way she presented herself to the world. How were her hips, tits, and piercings helping her?

Despite the nature of her double life, Jeanie decided to confide in her therapist. Well, her new therapist. Dr. Xavier announced his sudden and unexpected retirement days earlier, but Dr. Snow was eager to lend an ear and some warm advice. The female psychiatrist was familiar in a way Jeanie could not place, but she did not see the reason to press that thought further.

Dr. Snow did not question Jeanie's supersized confession, accepting her secret identity in stride. She wasted no time trying to be helpful. "Well, if you see this Miracles as gifts meant to make you a better hero, maybe you should think about the positives of these new changes in your life. Not all our blessings in life are obvious."

Jeanie closed her eyes and thought about her "blessings," failing to see what her lewd body was doing for her. Still, if these were Miracles, they had to mean something. Deep in her heart, she believed there was a purpose.

Each change was making her body "sexy." Before becoming Miracle Girl, Jeanie was a plain, unassuming journalist. She never put much stock in what people thought about her appearance, but she expected the opinions ranged from "unspectacular" to "who?" Jeanie did not invest in her appearance because it just did not matter in her life.

The Miracles, for whatever reason, were gifting Jeanie beauty. She suddenly had the kind of raw sex appeal she never cared about when she was a small-time reporter. Was this a reward for doing so much good?

Or maybe she was becoming beautiful *because* she was a hero. "Well, I guess I've never been so important. People never really looked at me before. Now they look at me a lot—even more after these changes."

"So people look to you now," Dr. Snow concluded. "It's important for people to look up to you, so maybe these 'Miracles' want to make sure the world is always looking at you? You're already a symbol of Justice, but maybe Beauty is part of your identity you should accept."

That was a new concept. "I guess I've never thought my looks were that important."

"Well, do you now? How do you feel when people look at you because you're sexy?"

There was a warm sensation in Jeanie's stomach as she reflected on all the times she almost came from pleasure knowing people were watching her body. Was she finally understanding why her body reacted so viscerally to attention?

Maybe it was shallow, or maybe her beauty was important. It was good to have beauty in the world, right? "Maybe I am supposed to be embracing this and making myself beautiful."

"I think that's a good instinct," Dr. Snow praised, setting down her notebook. "You should start exploring these impulses and work on your appearance. Don't be afraid to trust the little voice in your head telling you to embrace your sex appeal."

"Thank you, Doctor."

The Silver Queen, doing her best to hide her grin behind her Doctor persona, nodded. "Of course, dear. And if being ogled and observed makes you feel validated, perhaps we should allow you to dress to your comfort level for our sessions going forward."

Jeanie looked so thankful pulling her loose cotton top over her head to show off those udders of hers. Dr. Snow was really helping her open up.

IF THE MIRACLES WANTED her to strive for beauty, Jeanie had to trust Dr. Snow and explore beauty as self-care. She heard the voice in the back of her head.

Smooth.

Flawless.

Jeanie was hesitant when she booked her appointment; this was so out of her comfort zone and unlike her. Her colleagues at the newspaper would stare and some might judge her behind her back.

Despite her doubts, Jeanie committed. It had been two weeks since Jeanie's appointments and she could finally see the Botox setting in, smoothing her skin to perfection. Her flawless mask of a face was complimented by the plumpness of her lips after her injections.

Now that she saw herself in the mirror, she understood. That warm sensation of validation flooded her body and she finally saw it; she was a vision of beauty.

She was *THE* Vision of Beauty.

Chapter 8: Personal Training

Months passed since Jeanie embraced vanity as a virtue, and she was looking more beautiful than ever. People noticed the change in her, whether she was Jeanie or Miracle Girl. They saw the visible changes, but she was starting to carry herself with a confidence no one could deny.

Jeanie loved her body and her new face, but even if she accepted her natural and artificial beauty as a blessing, they were becoming a distraction in the field. Several thieves escaped her pursuit because she flew by a reflective surface and had to double-check her makeup and hair.

Jeanie needed to work on her discipline, and Dr. Snow agreed. Lucky for the heroine, Dr. Snow worked in her off time as a personal trainer. She was more than happy to assist in adjusting Jeanie's attitude!

Before meeting Dr. Snow, Jeanie thought she knew what a personal trainer was; some of her colleagues had guys at the gym who would lead them through their exercises.

Training with Dr. Snow was not about exercise and it was different than learning how to fight or use her powers. Dr. Snow focused on Jeanie's day-to-day life and started implementing strict rules focused on discipline and control. If Jeanie touched herself, which was easy to absent-mindedly do with her piercings, her hands were cuffed behind her back. When she did not follow the letter of the instructions she was given, she would be bent over and spanked. She was learning consequences, and that would improve her behavior and her discipline.

Jeanie arrived at a "training session" after work, her cheeks red. "My boss told me I misquoted an interviewee today."

"And?"

The redhead scrunched her nose. "I bent over his desk. It was so embarrassing when he asked what I was doing!"

"This is good," Dr. Snow muttered, accidentally musing to herself aloud.

Jeanie furrowed her brow. "It is?"

Dr. Snow caught herself, regaining her composure and, more importantly, her control. "Did you just question me?"

Realizing her mistake, Jeanie apologized and bent at the waist over the Doctor's lap. She shuddered when her skirt was lifted and her panties were pulled down, exposing her to the air.

Dr. Snow swiftly struck Jeanie's fat ass, letting it wobble in recoil after Jeanie gasped. "You've proven that your training is becoming second nature." Another smack, another cry of pain and pleasure. "You know you deserve discipline when you make mistakes."

"But I can't do that at wo—AH!"

Dr. Snow tutted, shaking her head. "I will write notes to all your superiors, letting them know that your therapist has requested special treatment to better help you with your self-actualization needs." The letter did not matter, of course; The Silver Queen would just alter the minds of Jeanie's bosses so they stayed in line with her training regimen. "Going forward, this is what you should expect from anyone in charge of you."

As a reminder, she laid one last heavy smack on Jeanie's fleshy cheek, now red from the disciplinary action. "Now let us move to the next steps of your training."

SINCE BEAUTIFICATION was an important part of Jeanie's journey, Dr. Snow took a special interest in how Jeanie maintained her appearance and her hygiene. Jeanie might have gotten her lips done, but she was told there was so much left to improve.

With a new face like hers, Jeanie could not leave the house without a flawless coat of makeup. Looking natural was not important; she had to look like a perfect doll.

When acrylic nails were proposed, Jeanie initially objected. Impractically long nails would make fighting and typing harder. After a firm spanking she corrected her attitude. She could compensate with telekinesis.

The night ended with Jeanie laying on her bed so Dr. Snow could help with her last hygiene treatment. Going forward, she would not go out in public with any body hair. Jeanie had shaved her legs and her trainer was shaving her bikini area to make sure no stray hair remained. They would get her scheduled for laser hair removal appointments until not a follicle remained below her chin.

She had to be a shining example for all the good girls of the world, and a good girl did not fight crime without a clean pussy. She got that now.

Chapter 9: Read a Thought, Lose a Thought, Be a Thot

Jeanie was progressing along better than The Silver Queen could have hoped. Physically, she was turning herself into quite a specimen. An obscene, cartoonish specimen, but that was the goal. With her pseudo-nemesis turning into the perfect picture of a bimbo, maybe it was time to start adjusting her... mentality to match.

THE MIRACLES WERE FOCUSED on perfecting Jeanie's appearance recently, but her favorite gifts were still the superpowers that started her new life. Being a telekinetic was great, and everyone loved a fire show, but if she had to pick her absolute favorite, telepathy was the hands-down winner. Being able to know when baddies were going to shoot at her made fighting easier. It even helped in her civilian life as a journalist, giving her insight into the hard-hitting questions she should ask.

Telepathy made Jeanie's life easier but learning how to control it was its own challenge. The power always required a lot of mental focus to get right and overusing it usually left her lightheaded.

Those effects were more noticeable lately. Jeanie chalked it up to how much of her mental bandwidth was going into fighting, fashion, and hygiene, tugging her focus in every direction. When she used her power to peek inside someone else's head, it left her own feeling sluggish.

The lightheaded feeling used to fade quickly, but it was lingering now. The more she flexed her telepathy, the more of a scatterbrain Jeanie became, forgetting meetings and losing track of escaping criminals. When she pushed herself too far, Jeanie would come out of a pleasant haze and realize she had been zoning out, vacant stare and parted lips, for tens of minutes at a time.

The telepath was able to piece together a link between her mind reading and her mental struggles. She rationalized that when she used her telepathy to sneak into other people's heads and read their thoughts, some of her own thoughts were being pushed out because her head was too crowded. It made sense enough for Jeanie to slow down and use her telepathy less.

Unfortunately, and perhaps predictably, she forgot this commitment and started using it again. She broke her rule to interrogate a frog-themed supervillain. In exchange for Tadpole's thoughts on the tastiness of flies, Jeanie's caution surrounding telepathy faded into mental mist.

Going about her life as normal, Jeanie pried into people's minds at her leisure, feeling like she was forgetting something important, but she was unable to put her finger on it, so she pressed on.

"JEANIE. JEANIE!"

The redhead's eyes went wide, bringing her back to her senses just in time to feel a small glob of drool fall from her puffy lips. She was sitting at her desk in the newsroom. She must have tried reading her coworker's minds to figure out what everyone was thinking of for lunch. Her thoughtless daze was interrupted by her editor. "Yes sir? Sorry, sir."

"How did your interview go?"

"My…" Jeanie racked her brain, trying to recall the interview he was talking about, but no luck. He reminded her that she scheduled an appointment with a very private foreign dignitary earlier that day. That appointment came and went with Jeanie oblivious to the seven emails she missed sitting at her desk.

Jeanie apologized profusely and begged for punishment and discipline, but this was more than being a space cadet and leaving her makeup in the office bathroom. Her editor did take the opportunity to smack her fat ass one last time, but a fuck up like this could not be swept under the rug.

Sadly, with Jeanie's head like this, it was probably time for her to take a break from journalism to work on her "mental health." As with most decisions in her life, that break was encouraged by an authority figure when her editor-in-chief placed her on "indefinite leave."

Chapter 10: Changing Career Paths

Jeanie loved being a reporter, but maybe losing her job was inevitable. Being a superhero was a responsibility far greater than reporting on news stories. She had to save people, *and* she had to find new ways to beautify for the public. Those obligations kept a lot on her plate.

Sadly, Miracle Girl did not get a paycheck, so unless her Miracles were going to give her food and shelter, she had to look for new work. She was smart, graduating from her classes with honors. Unfortunately, all the smarts in the world could not salvage her attention span and forgetfulness, which got her fired from two temp jobs.

The job hunt for a space cadet superhero was frustrating until Jeanie's therapist reminded her to use the gifts she was given to solve her problems. Jeanie could not use pyrokinesis or psychic powers on her resume, but she did have an obscenely sexual body. She had asked the Miracles to give her the means to sustain herself, but maybe they already took care of her and were just waiting for Jeanie to catch up.

Jeanie already got turned on when people saw her in less clothing than normal, and people paid lots of money to do just that on sites like OnlyGoons! With a fat ass and big pierced naturals, Jeanie might as well have been designed for porn sites. She could easily bring in enough money to keep herself afloat while maintaining a flexible enough work schedule for Miracle Girl to save the day whenever she was needed.

MiraculousBabe quickly amassed her own loyal following of perverts, especially after her Trainer offered to manage and promote her page. She questioned whether the name was too close to her hero name, but Dr. Snow assured her she was overthinking the name. Surely no one would connect a miraculous bombshell sex working redhead with the bombshell sex symbol redhead superhero Miracle Girl.

MUCH TO JEANIE'S SURPRISE, she loved her new job. Every day, she took pictures and videos and money started coming in. Once she had all her things recorded for the day, she would even DM subscribers and read comments. Her typing was slow because she usually kept a few fingers rubbing her pussy to address the horny need that came from people praising her and worshiping her body.

Jeanie did notice some people saying, "Doesn't she look like Miracle Girl to you?" but she was not worried. It was like Dr. Snow said: were people going to believe a superhero was fucking herself on OnlyGoons?

Work like this would have made the old Jeanie self-conscious, but she was on therapist's orders to own her sexuality. It was satisfying to get big tips just to sext people through the site. *Very* satisfying.

Then she saw an offer for... well, it was a lot of money. Suddenly, one of her DMs had her full attention.

MrShaw: Well, are you interested?

MiraculousBabe: I'm always interested in that many zeroes! But what is it for? Special video? Photo shoot?

MrShaw: Oh darling, I was thinking we could have a meeting for a more interactive experience.

MiraculousBabe: Oh?

MiraculousBabe: Oh! Well, I've never really offered THAT before...

Another message popped up with a number doubling the last number. Knowing the exact price point someone wanted to pay to fuck her was apparently a turn-on, because "MiraculousBabe" was knocking on the door of Mr. Shaw's penthouse within the hour. She did not even question why he suggested she wear "Miracle Girl" cosplay. Everyone had their fantasies!

Between being an OnlyGoons girl and an escort, Jeanie was going to be set up with enough cash to buy pretty things and fancy toys, which in turn, she could use for her new jobs. The more she fucked, the more she could be paid to fuck, like she found a sex cheat code!

Jeanie may have been an airhead, but she was smart enough to make lemons out of lemonade.

Chapter 11: Biggest and Boobiest is Best

In hindsight, the Miracles were surprisingly kind to Jeanie. They gave her powers, they gave her a sexy body, and they even let her get turned on by the sexual attention of others. People perceiving her and finding her hot was enough to get Jeanie all hot and bothered, so with her recent change in career paths, she got to spend most of her day in a perpetual state of arousal.

No one was everyone's type, (supposedly,) but most people found MiraculousBabe hot. She knew that because she was climbing the ranks of popularity on OnlyGoons and people had not stopped hiring her as an escort. Her "dance card" was full to the point where she was letting her sex work cut into crime-fighting time. That was okay, she rationalized with the help of Dr. Snow; police were around for the small stuff.

Jeanie knew sexual approval turned her on. What she did not expect was the way she viscerally reacted when someone did not find her sexy. Or at least, not as sexy as she could be. She saw the comment on her OnlyGoons:

BiggestGlob: I mean, she's okay. I've seen bigger tits on this app though.

Jeanie pouted, feeling surprisingly inadequate. That was a new sensation. Jeanie grew up looking plain, but she was always humble and lived with not being everyone's cup of tea. Now that beauty was an important aspect of her identity, being negged felt more like a personal attack. She WAS beauty. Everyone, including this Glob guy, should recognize that, but apparently some girls had bigger cans and that was a dealbreaker.

Thoughts of inferiority crept into Jeanie's mind, but almost like magic, she felt her favorite tingling feeling.

Jeanie quickly turned on her webcam as ecstasy overtook her and she started moaning. Pulses of pleasure started in her chest, with every nerve ending in her breasts firing off, spawning new endings to multiply the delicious sensations.

The pulsing pushed her tits out in all directions, adding pounds of flesh. Every pulse made her chest strain into a new cup size, exploding out into a weight and roundness no one would believe was real. For all she knew, maybe they weren't? Did she care?

The sensations subsided. The whole transformation was fast, but so overwhelming, it left Jeanie with a dreamy, absent smile. She sat in a puddle, her body still trembling as she realized her mystical breast augmentation made her cum. She grasped one hefty tit in her hand, gasping when she squeezed the hypersensitive titflesh.

Jeanie looked like a lewd cartoon drawn into life. That made her smile—as much as her puffed up lips could smile. Jeanie knew she could trust the Miracles to craft her body to suit her purpose. Being a sex object was part of her purpose now, and with tits like hers, no one else would be more objectifiable than MiraculousBabe.

Chapter 12: A Better, Sluttier Solution to Criminal Justice

Being a superhero was exhausting. Jeanie had to make OnlyGoons content, go to scheduled appointments to fuck strangers, and after all that, she still had to run around the city dealing with bad guys.

Jeanie needed a release, and she found it hitting bars and clubs. Not all the time! But like... once a week. She just ended up at a club, and she would have... well, a LOT of drinks. But it was only once a week! So not a problem!

Tonight, Jeanie was knocking out two birds with one stone. There was some gang meeting up at a club downtown. Miracle Girl made an appearance at the club so she could break up the meeting, bring in the gang members, and maybe get a few drinks in before she went home.

It was a flawless plan if not for her darn memory, which might have gotten worse with her recent drinking habits.

Miracle Girl got to the club, in costume and everything, but then she noticed the bar and thought she could use a drink. After about thirteen drinks and some dancing later, someone told the gang members Miracle Girl was trashed on the dance floor. They didn't believe it until they saw the heroine themselves.

Twerking on another girl on the dance floor, Miracle Girl eventually noticed a group of men watching her. They were reaching for weapons, and she realized they were a gang! Her booze-soaked brain managed to remember that gangs were, in fact, bad and she was the one who stopped them from doing gang things!

Miracle Girl leapt forward to give chase. The heroine immediately wobbled and tripped over herself.

She knocked a few bad guys back with telekinesis, but she did not trust her fire, so she tried chasing them through the back rooms of the building. She saw them turn into a room, so she stumbled into it, raised her hand—

And nothing. The room had something to inhibit meta powers!

The gang members bested her easily, because she was outnumbered and blitzed out of her mind. Jeanie had to think quickly, which was not her strong suit, with or without alcohol. But she was very good at thinking horny, and the room of muscular men made horny a strong emotion to draw from.

"Wait, wait, wait," Miracle Girl called out, confusing the criminals in the process of brandishing weapons. "You could totally be lame-os who fight and beat up a superhero, but people totally do that already."

Miracle Girl was answered by clueless expressions, but that changed when she started shimmying out of her skimpy hero costume. "How many goons can say they've fucked a hero?"

MAYBE FUCKING NAMELESS criminals was an out-of-the-box solution, but it was a solution Miracle Girl was perfectly equipped for. They clearly had a lot of pent-up-frustration, and instead of taking it out on unsuspecting citizens, her needy cunt was ready to shoulder the abuse.

The organization kept Miracle Girl at the club, satisfying a never-ending line of bad guys for three days straight. That was three whole days where they weren't on the streets causing crime!

Eventually, their boss got enough amusement out of the heroine and had his hirelings toss her out in the back alley behind the club. Jeanie's legs were weak and cum was still dripping down her thighs, so she grabbed her sticky costume and floated back to her apartment. After everything, she was overjoyed by the warmth of a job well done and a belly full of semen.

Chapter 13: Miracle Girl vs Silver Queen Round 2!

Emily was having a blast fucking with Jeanie's life, but the time for Miracle Girl to properly square off against her nemesis was long overdue. The media was reporting on Miracle Girl as a potential scandal, with her recent "boob job" and pictures leaking of her enthusiastically banging a major street gang. Her reputation was starting to pivot from an empowered heroine to a sex-crazed super bimbo, but the media was still unwilling to deny her abilities as a crime fighter.

The Silver Queen could finally start the process of showing the world, and maybe even Jeanie herself, who "Miracle Girl" truly was underneath it all.

WHAT WAS THE EASIEST way to get the bimbo hero's attention on a national stage? The Silver Queen just turned the city's football stadium into her own castle. The stands, once filled with former sports fans, were now lined with mindless subjects, loyally watching and masturbating in adoration for their queen.

The Silver Queen herself sat atop her throne in the center of the field, awaiting her jester.

On cue, Miracle Girl hovered down to the field, landing with a wobble. She really had come a long way from the plain redheaded telepath Emily picked out of the crowd. Her drinking habit had turned into a party hard lifestyle, often done in costume. The scent of tequila could be picked up from thirty yards off, and Emily was sure she saw a cum stain on the underbust corset framing those obscene breasts.

Miracle Girl stood tall, slurring her words out loudly. "Mish Silver Queen, I've come to free these shitizens from your grasp!"

"Have you?" Emily chuckled from the comfort of her throne. "With a body like that? I assumed you were here to strip down to entertain your queen. You've clearly been dying for attention, letting your tits get so big."

"But I didn't..." Miracle Girl shook her head, still feeling the lingering drinks in her head. She didn't pick out her tits, despite the news claiming she clearly went through some vanity surgery. "The Miracles—"

"You are the Miracles, you dumb little bimbo. It's in your name," The Silver Queen explained, stretching the truth. Much of what Jeanie had been given, part of her wanted deep down in her subconscious. Who didn't want a bombshell body? Each quiet dark desire could be plucked by a reality bender like The Silver Queen.

But like any monkey paw wish, what you got was not always what you expected. "You clearly wished this. Don't you enjoy those tits of yours? Didn't you want them bigger? You gave up your job and shame to become a ballooned-up sex doll, and I bet you'd give up more."

Miracle Girl wanted to argue, but the idea of being a living sex doll made her wet. Would she go back to her old job if she could? Was reporting anywhere near as fun as riding dildoes and fucking rich people? "I'm just doing what the Miracles made me for..." She was designed for sex. Was that really her choice?

The Silver Queen smirked. "I bet you'd give up your mind. You barely use it anyway, but you use your body a lot, don't you?" She whispered honeyed words, heard clearly by Jeanie despite their distance, like she was speaking directly into Jeanie's mind.

"Wish it, you know you want to. Drain away the IQ you don't need. Put it where it really matters."

Miracle Girl tried to argue, but she felt a tingle between her legs when The Silver Queen spoke. She wanted this, didn't she? She was a beacon of beauty for the city to stare at. Even now, with the crowd masturbating their support, she felt that desire cloud her head.

She imagined herself as more. And her head fogged up, thoughts and knowledge popping away like bubbles, feeding her body as her bubble butt became a shelf sticking out twice as far as her thighs. Her breasts... tits... titties! They were even more outlandish, growing well past the point where each one was greater than her own head, which felt more and more empty as inches were added. The straps of her costume snapped and the fabric tore, unprepared for the sex goddess Miracle Girl was becoming.

Miracle Girl's moans echoed across the stadium, caught on every camera littering the stadium. She did not care. Her thoughts were so clear now because they were so simple. She was a sexy body and everyone should see her become her true self, made of tits and ass and pure desire

"There now... how does that make you feel, Miracle Girl?" The Queen said, summoning her "nemesis" to the throne.

Miracle Girl looked at her, a dopey, absent expression devolving into giggling. "I'm here for you! Stoppin' you," she managed, each word a struggle. "By, um... I forgot?"

The Queen smiled, whisking away Miracle Girl's poor excuse for clothes with one flick of her wrist. "You're going to stop me by licking my pussy. You're going to show the world just how good you can worship my folds. You'll be so good at it, I'll be forced to free my thralls." And she might; she only needed so many fuck slaves back at the mansion.

The heroine's tongue lolled in her mouth as her eyes were drawn to the Queen's cunt. "Oh, gosh, you must be right. Well, I better get to work!" Miracle Girl got to her knees and buried herself between the Queen's toned thighs. Even her tongue was molded for sex now, long and wide. Along with her thick lips, it was slightly too big for her to ever talk without a lisp again, but it was perfect for brushing the Queen's nub and probing deep into her sweet cunt.

Chapter 14: Cunt Drunk

The run-in with The Silver Queen stuck with Jeanie. Honestly, it had been a rough couple of weeks for Miracle Girl. She had been captured by a gang of thugs, who she eagerly serviced, then her nemesis made a slutty fool of her on camera. The changes to her body and mind stuck with Jeanie, making her easily the dumbest hero around, and her peers and villains all knew it. Another hero demanded she take an "attitude test" or whatever, and by the end, he was asking if she had ever attended any kind of school at all.

Being dumb and forgetful made traditional crime fighting harder. Jeanie made bad decisions and fell into traps, and sometimes she went so far as to forget how to use her powers, entirely. Needless to say, she was caught by bad guys often.

Villains never killed her, though; they heard about her reputation. When she got caught, she'd often become the center of a henchman orgy. Sex was becoming Miracle Girl's most notable superpower, ending more crimes than her telekinesis and fire powers combined.

The longer Jeanie adjusted to this new normal, The Silver Queen's words stuck with her. These Miracles were just what Jeanie wanted. She wanted to be dumb. She wanted to be slutty. Deep in her core, she believed her nemesis had a point, because none of this felt "wrong."

Of course, there were other ways The Silver Queen and her delicious pussy stuck with Jeanie. After another night of failing to fight street-level thugs, Miracle Girl was unexpectedly rescued from a mob of villains mid-gangbang. Shady Kitten, a heroine from a nearby city, grabbed her and phased her through the wall, phasing three cocks out of Miracle Girl in the process.

When Jeanie came out of her sex haze, she was on a fancy plane with Kitten piloting. "You might need to stop with the heroing for a while, MG. We can't keep taking time out of our nights to save you from... um..." Other heroes could be so squeamish about sex.

"Bad guy gangbangs?" Miracle Girl giggled. "You don't have to save me; they always let me go when they're done."

Kitten blushed a deep red, not looking at the bimbo hero. "It gives the job a bad name. People are going to think heroes are just undercover sluts."

"But it's just me; and I'm not under covers. I'm naked," she pointed out, which did make Kitten look back at her on instinct, before turning around hastily. "But it was nice of you to save me, even if you grabbed me mid-fuck."

"Seriously?" Kitten could not wrap her head around Miracle Girl's priorities.

"Seriously! Maybe I should repay you... I am still all horned-up, after all." And while the parade of dick at the casino was satisfying, The Silver Queen had left Jeanie with a craving she had yet to satiate again.

"What? I... I mean, that would be wrong," she justified to herself, trying to play the role of the honorable hero. She had never even explored sex with women, much less... well, the kind of woman Miracle Girl was.

Her objections did not stop Miracle Girl from whimpering and whining. Being this close to an attractive woman like Shady Kitten was enough to put her back in heat. "Come on, how would it be wrong? I bet you all think about it. About me." She dropped her voice low, draping herself around Kitten's shoulders so her tits squished against the serious heroine's back. "I bet you saw the tapes of me between The Silver Queen's legs. Maybe you can let me know what a good girl tastes like...?"

A shudder ran down Kitten's spine as she considered the offer. The closer Miracle Girl got to her, pressing that slutty body against her, the more Kitten felt her own heat rising. Neither woman realized that Miracle Girl had created another Miracle, giving her potent pheromones that affected other women when she was horny. She just needed a taste of Kitten's pussy, and her Miracles helped Kitten understand her.

Saving Jeanie was taking up the valuable time of other heroes... so she told Jeanie if she was willing to stay in Kitten's apartment for a week, chained to the bed with an on-brand Kitten Collar, the phasing heroine would give her what she wanted. Jeanie eagerly accepted; she would say or do whatever she had to if it meant lapping up nectar from between a beautiful woman's legs.

Chapter 15: Super (Porn)Stars

Much of Jeanie's non-hero time was spent in her own apartment or traveling to clients' places, but she missed having an office to work in. She was never going to be a reporter again, but maybe she should walk down to her old workplace to say hi to her old work friends. They would be amazed to see how different she was from the mousy, meek redhead they used to work with.

The walk took a lot more out of her than usual. She looked down at her soft, pudgy stomach. It had been that way for a while, right? With her ass and titties giving her ridiculous hourglass proportions, a soft tummy and squishy thighs fit perfectly as signature aspects of her look. She used mind powers, so it wasn't like she had to be a paragon of strength; she was a paragon of beauty! Duh; when she thought if it like that, why would she be fit like the other, less curvy heroines?

Jeanie found her way back to her old building after a few wrong turns. She asked to be buzzed up to... not the office. The studio. Reality shifted and warped around Jeanie as her simplistic brain filled in the gaps of a past she vaguely recalled. She was used to forgetting things, but if she tried really hard, she could probably get the facts straight.

Why did she think she used to work in an office? She remembered something about newspapers. Why were there newspapers when she was not much of a reader?

Oh right! It was a bit! They were filming a video where she pretended to be a reporter. She remembered cameras and desks. She picked the job because it was almost wish-fulfillment; she always wanted to be a reporter growing up! She just... never got there. Yeah, the more she dug back into her empty brain for memories, the more she remembered dropping out of school and changing career paths.

Without the brains to break big stories, Jeanie leaned into a job more suitable for a big sexy slut like her. When she went into porn. She was a no-name porn actress when she discovered her powers. She didn't even worry about coming up with a new identity, because her Manager, Dr. Snow said it would be good for her career!

As a porn star and a heroine, Jeanie could brand herself as Miracle Ass! Sure, the prudish media teased her, but plenty of people loved her as the first adult entertainment superheroine. That was how she got so famous for fucking actors on camera and bad guys on the streets.

The last remnants of Miracle Girl's original memories started to fade as she realized what was happening. This was her big Miracle: her life was changing so she was always her true self. No silly lies about the smart, shy wallflower getting powers. She had always lived her best ho life, embracing her sexuality and never looking back. That thought was comforting as it faded, leaving only Miracle Ass and her perfect porn star reality.

IT WAS NICE COMING back into the studio. She thought she was fired, but that was just Jeanie being dumb and forgetful.

She took a break to focus on her OnlyGoons, but she was called back to star in "Overpowered Super Sluts III" with another woman, leashed to a nearby couch and built with similarly obscene proportions. Jeanie observed the delicious fucktoy of a woman hungrily. "Mmm, I get to film with her? Lucky! What can I do to get a pre-shoot taste, Miss...?"

One of the buff stagehands looked at the dazed woman in question, her tongue hanging out like a fuckmutt. "Princess? Oh, good luck. She's got no brain. She's just a dumb former hero we got loaned out by the lady funding this flick. Does whatever we tell her to like a good pup." He grinned, looking at the two bimbos. "But... well, if you're really hungry, I'm sure I can convince her that she needs some rehearsal time, just the three of us, right, Fuck Princess?"

The dim-eyed heroine once known as Blackwing nodded eagerly, thrilling a horny Jeanie. The stagehand shoved Princess' face down into the cushions of the couch, and the ex-heroine responded by shaking her ass eagerly. The caked-up pornstar wobbling for her in the ear was enough of an invitation for Miracle Ass to part Princess' legs and bury her face into the needy cunt.

With Jeanie bent over the arm of the couch to reach an angle where she could eat out her new co-star, her own fat ass was perfectly positioned for the stagehand to give her a smack. She moaned into Princess, spreading her own legs. She couldn't see what was happening behind her, but she soon felt the euphoric sensation of a thick, freshly lubed cock pressing into her ass.

She had some buff hunk pumping into her ass while her face was drenched by an obscene bimbo crying out in pleasure for her. Gosh, Jeanie fucking *loved* her work!

Chapter 16: Sex Doll

Jeanie was coming out of her latest party bender, still tasting the latest round of salty and sweet juices from the cocks and cunts she must have serviced at the bar. She looked around the street, not sure where she was supposed to go next. Home? The studio?

Her heeled feet started walking, compelled by a tingling in her core to take her somewhere. The tingling reminded her of her Miracles, but it resonated deeper. She was living her best life, partying, fucking, and being worshiped as the world's favorite sex object. Jeanie was close to living her true purpose, but something was missing. This tingle was guiding her to that missing piece of her purpose.

After a long walk of people whistling and catcalling their favorite superslut, Miracle Ass, Jeanie knocked on the door of a high-rise building. It was not her own modest apartment, and she did not recognize it as a client's house. She did forget things, so maybe her instincts were finally taking over.

The servants at the front desk expected her, letting Jeanie up to the penthouse where The Silver Queen was waiting. Somehow, Jeanie had walked right into the lair of the world's most sexy, powerful supervillainess! Jeanie stared at the scantily-clad baddie in confusion until the villain asked if she was there for a fight.

Jeanie stalled, fat lips hanging open without much to say. That made sense, right? The Queen was her nemesis. She was a villain and Miracle Ass was a hero! Maybe she was there for her final battle!

But wasn't she the one who showed Miracle Ass how she could trade her smarts for more titty and more ass? The Silver Queen shared the truth of the Miracles with her. Without The Silver Queen, Miracle Ass would have clung to her brains, not realizing they were holding her back. She needed to give up the unnecessary things that distracted her from being the perfect fuck.

Life was so easy now. She fucked strangers. She fucked for cameras. She fucked bad guys, who weren't doing bad things when they fucked her, which was totally heroic. Everyone joked that she was a sex doll, but wasn't she happier than ever that way?

The Silver Queen laid seductively in her bed, but she didn't need a long speech that would go over Jeanie's head. The girl was so close to getting there on her own. All she had to say was, "You know what you are."

The Silver Queen smiled like a hungry predator as she watched Jeanie's figure changed. The meager brain cells she had left converted into more fat to swell her tits and ass. Her soft, absurd body could not compare to how soft her mind was left as her dopey eyes crossed, looking at the Queen.

"I'm so glad you found your way back to me," The Queen purred.

And she did. With nothing left in her head, everything was clear to Jeanie. The Queen had guided her from the start. She was Dr. Snow. She was the one who trained her, encouraged her, and helped her understand that the Miracles were always meant to turn Jeanie into the perfect sex doll for her Owner. One The Silver Queen could fuck with the added satisfaction of knowing she thoroughly defeated and embarrassed Jeanie along the way.

When the villain whisked away her skirt, the brainless bimbo hero giggled but waited for The Silver Queen to beckon her closer to serve. Jeanie spread The Queen's folds with her fingers, forming her pillow lips into a perfect circle around the Queen's clit, sucking and teasing it with her tongue as her fingers pressed into her. The queen moaned, pleased with her new toy, letting the mindless ex-heroine lick her eagerly to her first orgasm.

The Queen's breath wavered when she chuckled, brushing her own finger across her dripping slit until it sealed and her clit grew out, leaving Jeanie staring at a thick, firm cock. Jeanie was surprised, but too dumb to question the transformation. She was just happy to see a cock so eager to fuck her, which was exactly what happened when The Silver Queen tossed Jeanie onto the bed—tits up so she could watch those balloons bounce as she claimed Jeanie's cunt for herself.

Jeanie only knew how to fuck and how to obey, and she was the best at both.

Epilogue: Big Plans

Jeanie rarely strayed from her new home between The Silver Queen's thighs all weekend. She was such a good little cuntlicker, Emily could have sworn she was feeling dumber from all the blood rushing out of her head to feed into the sensations of each orgasm her new pet gave her.

The difference was The Silver Queen's sex stupor passed in the afterglow. Emily was still brilliant and now, she was two-for-two. Dixie was her perfect new fuckpet, Princess, and Jeanie was the perfect hero-shaped bimbo doll. Why stop now when she was finally having fun again?

The Queen would give Jeanie back the barest semblance of intelligence so she could continue to live as Miracle Ass. She liked having Jeanie out in the world, showing them what a good hero could be, fucking herself on camera and practicing her own brand of sex-first heroism.

And when The Silver Queen called, Jeanie would return to her Owner and get her brain drained once more. Her true purpose was to be The Queen's sex doll, built to serve.

THERE WERE SO MANY heroes and heroines who needed to see their true purpose. The Silver Queen could help, and the thought made her drip with wicked desire.

Don't miss out!

Visit the website below and you can sign up to receive emails whenever Layla Rose publishes a new book. There's no charge and no obligation.

https://books2read.com/r/B-A-PBIWE-PZAWB

BOOKS 2 READ

Connecting independent readers to independent writers.

Did you love *Build-a-Bimbo Heroine: Miracle Girl*? Then you should read *A Super Bimbofication: Superiorgirl*[1] by Layla Rose!

[2]

The Silver Queen, a reality-bending villainess, listlessly longs for something to do with her immense powers that won't bore her to death.

Watching the tantalizing heroines of the world running around with their idealism, morals, and modest talents, she decides there are no better toys to play with.

When Cara Daniels isn't breaking big stories and an enterprising reporter, she stands as a beacon of morality and justice from the stars. To be an example for the people of Earth,

---

1. https://books2read.com/u/brMPNz

2. https://books2read.com/u/brMPNz

Superiorgirl needs to learn to be her best self. Little does she know that a lusty supervillain is tipping the scales, altering Cara bit by bit, remaking her in the Queen's ideal image of a superheroine.

What kind of slutty fate does the Silver Queen have in store for the galaxy's girl scout?

If you enjoy Cara's bimbofication journey, be sure to check out the previous books in The Silver Queen's Superharem series!

Read more at https://www.tumblr.com/cottonundiestf.

Also by Layla Rose

The Silver Queen's Superharem
Bimbofication of a Vigilante: Blackwing
Build-a-Bimbo Heroine: Miracle Girl
A Super Bimbofication: Superiorgirl

Watch for more at https://www.tumblr.com/cottonundiestf.

About the Author

Layla is a trans woman who has a thing for erotic transformations, bimbofication, and any story that can change someone into something sillier or more sultry.If you enjoy Layla's lewd content, follow her on Tumblr and BlueSky. Feel free to offer your support by showing her support links some love!

Thank you to DarkMoney1 for the Layla art!

Read more at https://www.tumblr.com/cottonundiestf.